Dear Parent:
Your child's love of reading starts here!

Every child learns to read in a different way and at his or her own speed. You can help your young reader improve and become more confident by encouraging his or her own interests and abilities. You can also guide your child's spiritual development by reading stories with biblical values and Bible stories, like I Can Read! books published by Zonderkidz. From books your child reads with you to the first books he or she reads alone, there are I Can Read! books for every stage of reading:

SHARED READING
Basic language, word repetition, and whimsical illustrations, ideal for sharing with your emergent reader.

BEGINNING READING
Short sentences, familiar words, and simple concepts for children eager to read on their own.

READING WITH HELP
Engaging stories, longer sentences, and language play for developing readers.

READING ALONE
Complex plots, challenging vocabulary, and high-interest topics for the independent reader.

ADVANCED READING
Short paragraphs, chapters, and exciting themes for the perfect bridge to chapter books.

I Can Read! books have introduced children to the joy of reading since 1957. Featuring award-winning authors and illustrators and a fabulous cast of beloved characters, I Can Read! books set the standard for beginning readers.

A lifetime of discovery begins with the magical words **"I Can Read!"**

Visit www.icanread.com for information on enriching your child's reading experience.
Visit www.zonderkidz.com for more Zonderkidz I Can Read! titles.

"Whatever your hand finds to do,
do it with all your might."
—Ecclesiastes 9:10

ZONDERKIDZ

The Berenstain Bears Get the Job Done

ISBN 978-0-310-76817-3

Requests for information should be addressed to:
Zonderkidz, 3900 Sparks Drive SE, Grand Rapids, Michigan 49546

Editor: Annette Bourland
Design: Cindy Davis

Printed in China

18 19 20 21 22 23 24 25 26 27 /DSC/ 10 9 8 7 6 5 4 3 2 1

I Can Read! BEGINNING 1 READING

The Berenstain Bears®

Get the Job Done

written by Jan and Mike Berenstain

It was spring in Bear Country.

That meant it was time

for spring cleaning.

Mama, Papa, Brother, Sister,

and even Honey all had jobs to do.

The Bears got right to work!

Mama hung up the rugs to clean.

Papa went to fix the railing

on the front steps.

Brother, Sister, and Honey

had to clean

the playhouse in the backyard.

They all got off to a good start.

The sun was shining.

The air was fresh.

Birds were singing.
Bright flowers bloomed
in the garden.

Mama whacked at the rugs.

Huge clouds of dirt flew out of them.

Papa used his tools.

He carved a piece of wood into

the right shape for the railing.

Brother, Sister, and Honey
had brooms and brushes,
cloths and mops, buckets of water,
and soap.

First, they were going to sweep out the playhouse.

"Uh-oh!" said Brother,
looking inside. "Spiders!"
Sister and Honey peeked inside.

There were big, hairy spiders.

“Yuck!” they all said.

“Let’s not sweep out the inside,”
said Brother. “Let’s scrub the outside.
Maybe that will scare the spiders.”
So that’s what they did.

Then Brother spotted
an old baseball, a bat,
and a glove behind the playhouse.

Brother picked up the ball.

Sister picked up the bat.

Brother tossed the ball to Sister.

She hit it.

“You be the outfielder, Honey,” said Brother. He gave her the glove. Honey crawled through the grass and sat down.

Back at the tree house,

Mama and Papa were hard at work.

Mama was almost done with the rugs.

Papa was finishing the railing.

He stood up and stretched.

Papa saw Honey
sitting in the middle of the yard.
"What is Honey doing there?"
thought Papa.

A baseball landed
near Honey.

She picked it up and threw it.

"Hmmm!" said Papa.

Papa walked around the tree house.

He saw the cubs playing baseball.

Their brooms, brushes, cloths, and mops

were on the ground.

“This doesn’t look like
spring cleaning!” said Papa.
Brother and Sister tried to hide
the ball and bat.

Papa looked at the dirty playhouse.

“You did not clean at all!” said Papa.

“There are spiders in there!”

said Sister.

Papa smiled. He knew how scary

spiders can be.

"I'll get the spiders out,"
said Papa. "Then you can
get the job done."

Papa chased the spiders away.
Then Brother, Sister, and Honey
got to work.

Mama came to see what was going on.
She saw the cubs hard at work.
"The Bible says to enjoy your work,"
said Mama.

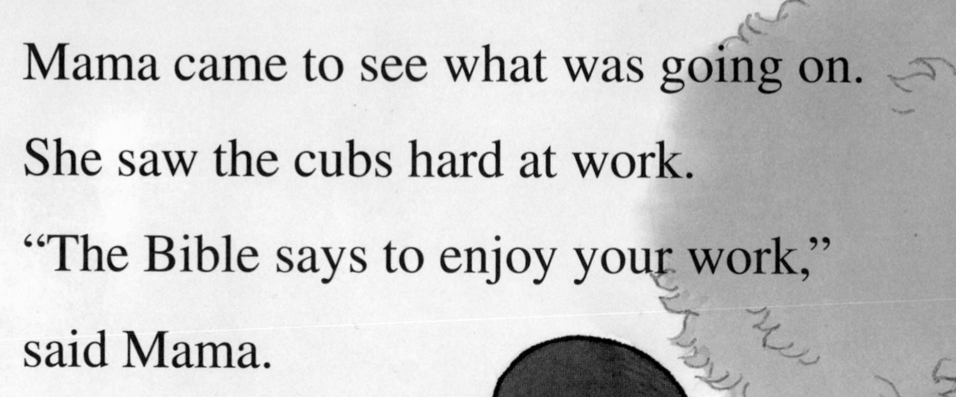

“Did you enjoy your work, Mama?”

asked Brother.

“I enjoy my clean rugs,” she said.

“And you will enjoy your clean playhouse.”

"We will enjoy it," said Sister.
"But without those spiders!"
It was a job well done.